Just Like Us

Just Like Us

HIAWYN ORAM

Pictures by DANIEL BAIRD

MOREHOUSE-BARLOW
78 DANBURY ROAD, WILTON, CT 06897

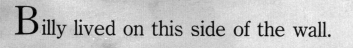
Billy lived on this side of the wall.

c.1/5/89

"Why can't I go and play on the other side?" he asked.

"Because very wicked people live there," said his mother, putting Billy's brother and sister into the laundry basket so she could have some peace and quiet. "And if you don't believe me ask your father."

Billy went to see his father in his laboratory.

"Why can't I play on the other side of the wall?"

"Because very wicked people live there," said his father, who was busy releasing a cloud of poison chemicals into the atmosphere. "And if you don't believe me ask your aunt."

Billy went to see his aunt at her breakfast of rabbits' hearts and sparrows' livers.

"Why can't I go and play on the other side of the wall?" he asked.

"Because terribly wicked people live there," said his aunt. "They'll have your ears for supper and your toes for lunch. And if you don't believe me ask your uncle."

Billy went to see his uncle in his new plastic greenhouse.

"Why can't I go and play on the other side of the wall?" he asked.

"Because very wicked people live there," said his uncle, who was trying to put some taste into his tomatoes. "And if you don't believe me I'll lock you up in my greenhouse for a week."

Billy went out to play on this side of
the wall.

"I see you've made a hole just big
enough for a boy to fit through," said
Miss Pritty, Billy's teacher, who happened
to be passing at that moment.

"It made itself," said Billy.

"Of course it did," said Miss Pritty.

Billy waited till Miss Pritty had
disappeared over the horizon.

Then he climbed through the hole in the wall.

"Hi," said a voice.

"Hi," said Billy.

"What's your name?" said the voice.

"Billy," said Billy, "what's yours?"

"Billy," said the other Billy.

Billy went with Billy to his secret hideout on the other side of the wall.

"I've got two brothers and two sisters and a dog," said Billy.

"Just like me," said Billy.

Billy walked with Billy to the end of town
on the other side of the wall.

"I'd get you a jawbreaker, only they
forgot my allowance again," said Billy.

"And mine," said Billy.

Billy took Billy fishing on the old canal on the other side of the wall.

"I'm no good at math, and I'm quite afraid of the dark," said Billy.

"Just like me," said Billy.

Billy climbed with Billy to the top of the tallest tree on the other side of the wall.

"When I grow up I'm going to marry Miss Pritty," said Billy.

"Me too," said Billy.

Billy walked with Billy back to the hole in the wall.

"Where are all the terribly wicked people?" asked Billy.

"On the other side of the wall," said Billy.

"Just like ours," said Billy.

Billy went home to his house on this side of the wall.

His mother and father and aunt and uncle were waiting for him.

"Billy," they ranted, "you've been to the other side of the wall."

"Yes," said Billy.

"With all those wicked people!"

"Yes," said Billy.

"Well," they raged, "and what were they like?"

"Just like us," said Billy.